For Ron —

Wishing you grand morning

walks of your own.

Thanks so much for sharing your

eagles with us. It's a treat I'll always

remember

Cheers, Joanne

(Ryder) 2/2000

Mockingbird Morning

by Joanne Ryder

illustrated by Dennis Nolan

Four Winds Press

New York

Special thanks to Jocelyn for walking through the morning—D.N.

Printed and bound in Japan. First American Edition   10   9   8   7   6   5   4   3   2   1

The text of this book is set in 16 point ITC Garamond Book Condensed. The illustrations are rendered in watercolor.

Library of Congress Cataloging-in-Publication Data
Ryder, Joanne.   Mockingbird morning/by Joanne Ryder;
illustrated by Dennis Nolan.—1st American ed.   p.   cm.
Summary: Poems take the reader on an early morning walk
to observe the animals of woods and water in happy solitude.
ISBN 0-02-777961-0
1. Animals—Juvenile poetry. 2. Nature—Juvenile poetry. 3. Children's poetry, American.
[1. Animals—Poetry. 2. Nature—Poetry. 3. American poetry.] I. Nolan, Dennis, ill. II. Title.
PS3568. Y399M63   1989   811'.54—dc 19   88-21305   CIP   AC

To Terry Moogan and Elly Kover
who watch and listen and enjoy walking together:
Happy days!—J.R.

For my father, who sang in the morning—D.N.

Outside your window
mockingbird is singing,
borrowing his song
from a hundred different birds,
calling to the empty morning
in a hundred different ways,
I am here. I am here.
Happy day! Happy day!

You pluck the peach
all warm and ready
from the windowsill
and eat your breakfast
with the sparrows.

The summer wind
tickles brown feathers
tickles your face
and the peach
soft and sweet
tickles you
inside.

Two doves
slowly search
the grass for food
never far apart,
their soft voices
gently touching:
I am here. You?
Here. And you?
I am here. You?

You kick
three brown leaves
and discover
a hole
leading down
to dark places
you cannot see.

You look down
and wonder
if someone
is looking up
wondering
about you.

Under the trees
the moss
is like a quiet animal
waiting
for you to come
and touch
its softness.

Feel its fur gently.
Listen…
you can almost
hear it purr.

A box
lies
in the woods
unopened.
You touch it
but cannot
break the spell.
You sit beside it,
not moving,
wishing
it would open.

Slowly
a crack widens.
Claws stretch,
a hairless head
creeps out,
and turtle
watches you
with bright red eyes.

A crooked tree
leans over the water.
Its long leafy branches
droop like a curtain
hiding you
from the other side
of the pond.

This is your place,
but today
goose is here first
smoothing her feathers
pecking out old ones
she no longer wants.

At last,
goose slides
into the water
swimming through
the leafy curtain
into the big room
beyond.
For a while
the tiny tree room
is yours,
and so is
one long brown feather
tucked in the grass.

Several tiny suns
flicker on the water
brightening
your tree room.

Look up
and watch
the pond light
dance along
the tall dark
branches.

Look down
and watch
pond patterns
ripple across
your smooth brown
arms and legs.

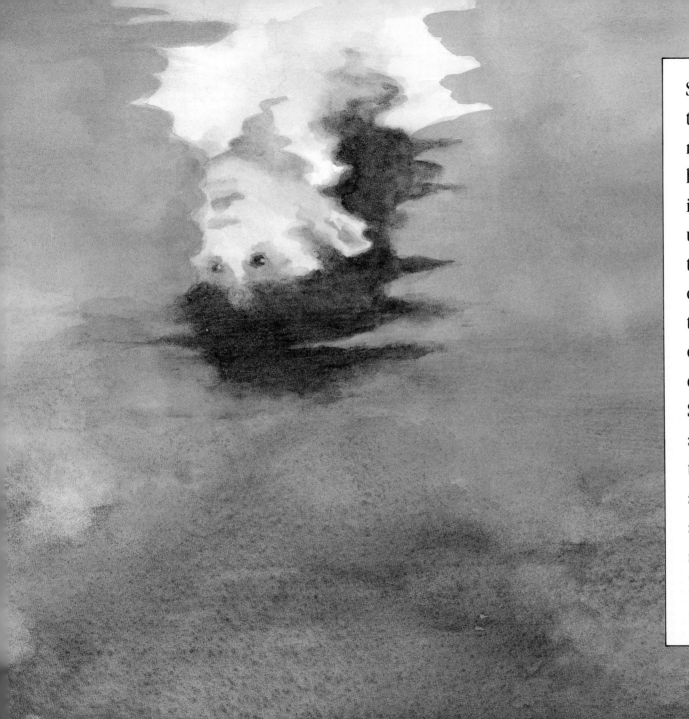

Someone enters
the pond room
moving so silently
her visit
is unnoticed
until you see
the flash
of golden scales,
the swirl
of pale fins
deep in the water.
She tugs
at muddy roots,
then leaves
as quietly
as she came,
a golden treasure
hidden
again.

Like magic,
thin green sticks
rise from the weeds
soar over the water
and stop,
hanging in
sunny space.
You wonder how
the trick is done
until you see
long wings
clear as glass.
And if you had
one wish today,
you'd ask for
dragonfly wings
in just your size
to surprise
to surprise.

Lying on the grass
you watch
a chase
in slow motion—
a shark
chasing
a cat
chasing
a boat
chasing
a kangaroo
floating
beyond reach.

When you reach
the sitting rock,
lizard slides off,
robin races by,
and someone leaps,
hiding behind
the tall bushes.

Only ant creeps
toward you,
accepting
the soft
hairy hill
that changes
her path.

Small round moons
rise
above the grass.

Bees
in fat fuzzy suits
wander
like astronauts
from moon to moon
touching down
crashing softly
making each
moon
dance
and
dance.

You find the path
where the grass parts,
where your feet
know the way
by themselves.

You feel
the warm sun
toasting you
outside.
Inside you,
summer pictures
flicker in your mind:
leafy curtains open
and tiny creatures
leap and creep
and swim silently
keeping you company
all the way
home.

Outside your window
mockingbird is singing
something old, something new
in a hundred different voices,
We are here. We are you.
We are here. You are we.
Happy day! Happy day!